Enid Blyton™

TOYLAND™ STORIES

BIG-EARS TO THE RESCUE

This edition first published in Great Britain by HarperCollins Publishers Ltd in 1998

1 3 5 7 9 10 8 6 4 2

Copyright © 1998 Enid Blyton Company Ltd. Enid Blyton's signature mark and the
words 'NODDY' and 'TOYLAND' are Registered Trade Marks of Enid Blyton Ltd.
For further information on Enid Blyton please contact www.blyton.com

ISBN: 0 00 136082 5

Cover design and illustrations by County Studio

Printed and bound in Singapore

Enid Blyton™

TOYLAND™ STORIES

BIG-EARS TO THE RESCUE

Collins

An Imprint of HarperCollins*Publishers*

One morning, Big-Ears was woken by a
PITTER-PATTER on his window.
"Oh, bother!" he grumbled. "It's raining again."
It had rained in Toyland
for days and days.

Big-Ears got out of bed and looked out of his
window. All he could see was water. Toyland
was flooded!

"I won't be able to go out again today!"
moaned Big-Ears. "The water is too deep,
even for wearing wellingtons!"

He felt very sad. It was so long since
he had seen any of his friends.

"Ah well," Big-Ears said to himself. "It's going to be another quiet day at home for me!"

He got dressed and was just about to make breakfast when he heard a loud **DRIP.**

Big-Ears looked up, and something plopped in his eye. It was a raindrop.

"Oh no!" he cried. "My roof must be leaking!"

Big-Ears found a bucket and placed it on the floor to catch the water. He was about to make his breakfast again when he heard another drip. He spotted a puddle on the floor. Then another. And another. His roof must have *lots* of holes which were letting in the rain.

Poor Big-Ears had to rush around finding as many pans and bowls as he could. He placed them all on the floor to catch the drips.

"I hope it stops raining soon," he said wearily. "Because I don't have anything else to catch the water in!"

Big-Ears flopped into his armchair. He was very tired from rushing about so much. Suddenly he heard a **splashing** and a **swishing** outside his window.

"Whatever is that?" he wondered.

He turned round. First he saw Sammy Sailor's head bobbing past his window. Then Sally Skittle's and then Noddy's.

He got up to look out of the window and he saw that they were in rowing boats! Sammy Sailor and Sally Skittle were in one boat. Behind them in another was Noddy. A rope was fastened between the two boats keeping them together.

"How wonderful!" laughed Big-Ears, clapping his hands. "A boating trip!"

"Big-Ears, we need your help!" said Noddy anxiously.

"Some of my poor little children fell over in the rain," sobbed Sally Skittle. "And they've been swept away in the flood."

"We need someone clever like you to help us find them," said Noddy.

"Well," said Big-Ears, "I'll go in one boat with Noddy, and Sally and Sammy Sailor can go in the other boat. That way we can look in different directions."

"Oh, Big-Ears, you are so clever!" said Noddy.

But then Big-Ears remembered that he couldn't go out through his door.

The water would flood inside his house, and he had more than enough rain inside already!

He opened the window
and squeezed through.
Big-Ears landed in
Noddy's boat with a
THUD!

The boat
rocked and
the water splashed
but soon he
was settled.

"We'll look in the Dark Wood for your children, Sally," he called. "Don't worry, we'll find them. I'm sure they'll be safe."

Big-Ears took command of the oars and soon he and Noddy were rowing slowly towards the Dark Wood. It was very dark. Water dripped through the trees. Birds screeched in the shadows.

All of a sudden, there was a strange shrieking
and wailing. Noddy and Big-Ears jumped
with fright.

"What's that?" asked Noddy nervously.

"I don't know," replied Big-Ears. "But we must
be brave for the sake of Sally Skittle's children."

They began to row towards the hollow where the sound was coming from. They peeped anxiously between the trees. There they saw the Skittle children splashing and playing in the water. Noddy and Big-Ears had heard the sound of their laughter echoing through the wood.

Big-Ears rowed up to the children and pulled them into the boat.

"Your mother will be pleased to see you," Big-Ears told them. "She has been very worried about you."

Back at Toadstool House the rain had stopped and
Sally Skittle and Sammy the Sailor were waiting.

"Thank goodness the rain has stopped," said
Big-Ears as he opened his door. "I think we all
need a nice warm cup of cocoa."

But when
Big-Ears went
to look for a pan
to warm the milk,
he couldn't find
one. They were
all on the floor
full of rainwater!

"I'd forgotten all about
my leaking roof," he sighed.
"Don't worry," said
Sammy Sailor. "I'll mend
it for you."

Big-Ears smiled. That morning he had felt miserable. But now he was happy because his friends were here. And they were here because of the flood. Maybe the rain wasn't so horrible after all!

THE NODDY CLASSIC LIBRARY
by *Enid Blyton*™

Available in hardback
Published by HarperCollins